The Secret Life of Golf Balls

Story and Pictures by Katie Jarrett

For Clint,

Your story inspired

"The Secret Life of Golf Balls".

For Gray,

You never know how one day can change the rest of your life.

Today was going to be another beautiful day on the golf course.

The sun was shining with just the right amount of clouds in the sky to provide some shade.

The wind was just right; not blowing too far East, not blowing too far West, just blowing enough to give the guys a little extra push.

Bart, Stew, and Larry were walking up to the golf shop, ready to start the workday.

With a few minutes to spare before they had to clock in, the boys starting chatting about the day while sipping on their coffee.

"I hope we get some good players today! I sure am wanting to fly far!" said Bart excitedly.

"I can't wait!" agreed Stew.

Larry, on the other hand, was a bit nervous. He just pictured the sign in the golf shop that read

"Missing golf balls. Call if found!"

He was scared to end up lost somewhere along the trees, lonely and afraid to never be found.

Everyone dispersed to their stations; today, Bart and Stew would be working the driving range and Larry would be out on the course.

The balls would alternate between the golf course and the driving range. The driving range was always a bit more promising to get some good hits in; it was not always guaranteed you would be used when working the course.

CJ and his dad walked into the golf shop.

"Dad, I don't really want to play today. It's boring here; I'd rather go play my videogames," said CJ.

"CJ, I promise you just need to give it a try. The day is beautiful, warm sunshine, nice breeze. A perfect day to spend outdoors. You never know what might happen on the golf course; you could see some wildlife, you could get a hole in one, you may just have a great time," responded CJ's dad.

The golf balls on the counter were super excited to see CJ and his dad come in, hoping they would get picked up to play today.

Larry, however, sat on top, worried as ever, hoping he would not go out on the course today.

CJ's dad handed him a few dollars and told him to go get a bucket of balls at the ball dispensing machine.

CJ walked over to the ball dispensing machine and inserted his money. Out came the golf balls flowing into the basket. If it had not been for the loud noise the machine made, CJ would have heard Stew and Bart hooting and hollering with excitement as they came tumbling out.

CJ walked over and met his dad at their spot on the range.

He grabbed his driver, took a ball out of the basket (little did he know he grabbed Bart), and placed it on the tee.

After doing a few practice swings, he lined up next to the tee, and gave it all he could with his swing.

The excited shouts from Bart were muffled by the driver making contact with the ball.

Bart darted through the air,
excited to feel the warm wind.

Before Bart knew it, Stew had dropped into the soft grass just beside him.

"What a ride!" said Stew excitedly. "Hope we get collected for a second round this afternoon!"

After CJ and his dad finished hitting their bucket of balls, they made their way to their car to head home.

As they were walking to their car, CJ spotted a lonely ball that looked like it had been forgotten by the trees near the parking lot.

Looking around to make sure it was not anyone's ball, CJ scooped up the ball and put it in his pocket.

He was not going to let a lonely golf ball be left behind; no one would ever find or play this ball again, being lost all the way out here.

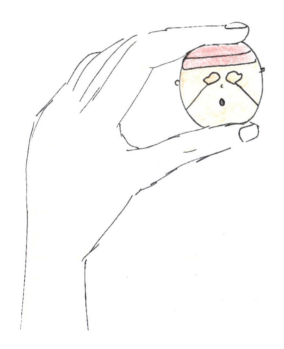

Larry, on the other hand, was scared and covered his eyes in fear.

That night, CJ was putting around in his room with the golf ball he had brought home earlier from the golf course.

CJ dropped the ball on the floor and grabbed his putter. As he went to gently putt the ball into his practice hole, he heard a cry for help. He looked around and could not figure out where that cry had come from.

Thinking he imagined it, he went to putt the golf ball in the hole again, when he heard the cry again. This time he knew it was real.

CJ looked down at the golf ball. He muffled to himself that the golf ball could not be crying out for help. Just as he finished convincing himself he was hearing things; the golf ball spoke up even louder.

"Please help me!" the golf ball shouted. "My name is Larry; can you take me back to the golf course?"

"Hi Larry, my name is CJ," replied CJ. "I'm sorry I brought you home from the golf course, I guess I just thought you had been left behind."

Larry replied, "Yes, we do get left behind and lost!"

Then Larry told CJ all about the missing golf balls that are forgotten by the trees and the missing golf ball posts he sees at work every day.

"I'm sorry for taking you from your course Larry. I will bring you back first thing tomorrow morning,"

"I'll bring my friends too, so they can help find your missing buddies," said CJ.

With that promise, CJ tucked Larry into his practice hole so he could feel at home. Larry drifted off to sleep, feeling good about returning to the course tomorrow and reuniting with his friends.

The next day, CJ was back at the golf course with his friends.

Together, they walked through all the areas where golf balls could have been forgotten and missed, collecting them as they went along (making sure that they did not belong to anyone playing today, of course).

As the friends picked up golf balls, they would play them on the course. The golf balls were happy once again, instead of being lost and left behind.

Larry was happy because he not only was saved from turning into one of those pictures on the missing golf balls signs, but he was also reunited with his friends that he had not seen for months.

As the years passed by, CJ and his friends continued to play golf and collect the missing golf balls that everyone else had left behind, giving the balls more chances on playing the course.

In exchange for all the help CJ provided, Larry gave CJ pointers to improve his golf game

"Always remember CJ, head down, eye on the ball," Larry would remind him as they practiced.

The two became the best of friends as CJ continued to play. He enjoyed the game of golf so much that he ended up becoming a PGA Professional; teaching others how to play golf.

CJ felt fortunate he got to do something he loved, every single day, as his job.

This was all thanks to that one day that changed the rest of his life; coming to play golf and finding out the secret life of golf balls.

THE END

Made in the USA
Monee, IL
25 April 2025

16358576R00026